THE REFUGE

Prequel to the Xianova Chronicles

Jen Porter

SNS Publishing, LLC

www.jenporterauthor.com

To all who wonder if God still speaks to us

~1~

"This way!" a man's voice hissed, much closer than the shooters. Tahni jumped. Was she just hearing things in the crackling of the many tiny smoldering fires all around her?

She frantically scanned the jungle's smoky understory. Another Tesla blast zinged past the immense tree trunk that protected her. She heard one of the shooters at a distance, signaling his team. More monkeys screamed as the resident troop fled the area. She looked again, more slowly, trying to locate the nearer voice.

There he was. A Herculean man waved from behind another tree's buttress root, about fifteen feet behind her. *Zzzzap!* A nearby fig vine snapped like a burnt rubber band and swung past her shoulder. She pressed back into the tree. Her leather boots sank into the damp soil.

The man pulled back out of sight. Several blasts in succession tore through nearby vines and singed more of her tree and the undergrowth; the sound was deafening. The onslaught of smoke choked her like tear gas. She swallowed hard and pulled her shirt up over her mouth and nose to keep from coughing.

It had to be a trap. She'd seen him with the raiders just a few minutes before. No way she could risk trusting him.

She had cover in this dense undergrowth, but the lightning gun blasts were all too close to the mark. She crouched and ran, angling away from him and the other raiders, weaving and scrambling to escape the immediate onslaught from the raiders' guns.

She ducked behind a smaller tree just as a blast hit it, smoke rising from a new burn. They had to have a tech genius in their ranks; Impures should not be able to fire the DNA-locked Tesla rifles.

Tahni crawled to another large tree, got up, and darted to another. No sign of the colossus.

She darted, ducked, crawled, and squirmed away in a random pattern for several minutes, until the plasma beams became more erratic, no longer zinging around and past her every time she moved. Her ears were ringing. Her breathing was too loud. She army-crawled into a heavy growth of tall ginger plants and pressed herself flat to the ground. Her heartbeat deafened her as it beat against the cool mud and mulch.

An immense boa slithered by, far too close for comfort. Thankfully, it was in a hurry to get away, too.

A minute later, the gunfire stopped completely. A deep roar echoed in the distance, and another one answered. Atrox lions? Great. Raiders, genetically-modified prehistoric predators... All would be on her trail soon.

She lifted her head slightly and swiped her left forearm to access her bio. The small holographic display told her the rendezvous point was less than a mile away and gave her a route free of known man-eating constrictor vines. She closed it.

There was no time to figure out how to lose these raiders. They were too good. The well-trained guardsmen she'd planned to ditch while "relieving herself" had been killed and looted within minutes of being attacked, just as she stepped away. She'd barely escaped the initial slaughter when they realized she was not among the dead.

She inched slowly toward another kapok tree, trying not to disturb the ginger stems as she passed. Thankfully, a slight breeze helped disguise her movement. She stood up in some tall ferns behind the enormous trunk, worked her way around to the other side, and peeked out.

An enormous hand clamped tightly around her mouth and pulled her back. She thrashed, twisted, and tried to drop to the ground. The giant held her head securely against his body with embarrassingly little effort.

"Stop!" He whispered directly into her ear. He pointed in the direction of the rendezvous point. "I can get you there safely." He let go of her mouth slowly, then motioned for her to follow him as he slid off into the shadows, his huge form somehow becoming one with them.

He knew where she was going.

Despite the many dangers — which usually made a quick end of anyone insane enough to leave the Xianovan dome system without trained guardsmen — she had to go this last short leg alone. No one could know that Nyk, Alin, and Cyril were alive. But how would she lose this guy?

She followed.

Coryl didn't know why he felt it necessary to help this woman escape from Gaspaar's crew. But here he was, leading her to where he knew she was headed: the clandestine landing site of the magnacutter in the jungle. He was probably the only witness to the ending of that cleverly faked crash. Saving the boy, no doubt. More Impure emigrants from Xianova, fleeing the "Blessing" of waiting for an unlikely cure in cryogenic storage in space.

He slipped through the jungle, leaving almost no trace, keeping a close eye on the woman behind him. The dream drifted into his mind again...but he pushed it out, physically stopping and purposefully surveying his surroundings.

The path he'd chosen was littered with fallen and rotting leaves and bark, low growth of vines and weeds, and other debris – good for keeping their footprints from the damp, muddy soil underneath. Just enough light filtered through the canopy above to keep him oriented. Frogs croaked. The sound of rustling leaves indicated the presence of more small animals in the trees. A variety of birds flew back and forth above him, calling. As he watched, a bird landed on a thick vine in front of him, and was immediately snatched and 'popped,' then enveloped to be digested later.

Coryl blinked away sweat as it stung his eyes, holding very still. This constrictor vine was a newer one, as yet unmarked in the geotagging system. He scrutinized the vine's spread carefully, hoping he wasn't already in range. No, but close. He'd almost walked right into it.

He turned and waited for the woman to look at him, and mimed a choke hold, pointing at the thick curlicue of hungry tendril drooping from the branches ahead. He altered his course to give it a wide berth as he moved forward, and she followed him.

He had dreamed the same dream several times, of late. Fragments of it seeped into his consciousness day and night, leaving behind a clinging dread.

Why did he feel *so* compelled to help this family? It only served to endanger his tenuous collaboration with Gaspaar. And his life.

The woman in his dream was not this woman, but somehow, he *knew* they were connected. This woman must live.

Or his son would die.

~2~

"Tell me a story!" Solin demanded as he climbed up into a chair next to Kurn's. Kurn smiled, but the smile didn't reach his eyes.

His son was so smart, so advanced for such a tiny little boy. But his impurity was becoming too obvious, and his screening was coming up. Was he old enough to know the real truth about why his father had to leave?

Kurn sighed. He would be gone tomorrow, but if all went well...

"Ok, Solin. Daddy will tell you about where the Blessed Ones, like Uncle Kural, go.

"Ancient astronauts built the giant orbital ring in the sky. You can see it, out the window. Look." Kurn pointed to the window next to them, and Solin looked out at the evening sky, dim and dark beyond the lit-up world inside the transparent Dome. Kurn pointed at a solid band of lights among the dimmer stars in the sky.

"That big straight line of stars? The one that goes straight over the Central Spire building? That's the ring."

"Does it have buttons-n-joysticks and maybe a touchscreen?"

"Probably bajillions of them."

"Whoa. Doot doot doot!" He pushed imaginary buttons on the wall, the arm of Kurn's chair, Kurn's leg, and in the air, dancing around in his own little version of heaven.

"Solin, do you want to hear the rest?"

"People in the sky. Cold as icicles. Jooooy sticks! Yes!"

"At first, the astronauts thought they were building a new place to live —to save some of the people, because the Earth was dying. You remember why the world was dying?"

Solin nodded. "There were 10 thousand bajillion people!"

"Right! I'm impressed you remembered that 'exact' number," Kurn chuckled. "As it turned out, the ring wasn't finished before the Bio World War started. But it was finished enough. Some of the richest people escaped to it and froze themselves so they could live until after the war. But some of them were already sick, even though they didn't know it. Over and over, the sick ones were kicked out from their units. They got into fights, and the war kept going on in the sky—"

"Over and over and under and under."

"What do you mean, Solin?"

"The war, obviously."

"Yes, son, totally obvious." Kurn rolled his eyes and stifled a cringe at his son's injection of another string of his favorite words, but he'd humor him one more time. "Over and over and under and

under, obviously, but Daddy also meant again and again —
they fought and fought, obviously."

Solin bounced up and down on his tiptoes, flicking his
hands, loving the repetition.

"Because of all the fighting, they made locks for their doors
with codes that were so awesome that some sections are still
locked, even today."

"Codes-codes. 12345, 54321. Touch the touchscreen, or
touch the buttons?"

"I don't know, Solin. Probably a touchscreen *and* some buttons. Maybe even a dial. Or an eye scanner."

"...*and* some buttons *and* s'more buttons...doot doot doot."
He punched imaginary buttons in the air. "PSSSSHT. Door
OPENED!"

"There could still be people living in the ring behind some of
those locks! Someday Daddy wants to find out."

"Daddy goes DOOT DOOT DOOT PSSSHT! DOOR
OPENED! OUT PEOPLE!" Solin ran in a big circle around the
living room, waving his arms. "GET OUT PEOPLE! BACK
TO EARTH!"

"That would be great, if Daddy could do that...

"But other parts of the ring, they got unlocked, and they cleaned
and cleaned a long time later. Those are the sections where the
Ascenders take the Blessed Ones. When someone gets a Blessing,
like Uncle Kural, they go to those stars, to the ring, to wait for their
cure so they can come home again. When Daddy misses Uncle

Kural, I just look up to those stars, and I know Uncle Kural isn't dead; I might get to see him again someday."

"But *they* don't come back, never."

"Sometimes they do."

"Nope, never-na-never-na-never!"

"Ok, now. Solin, Daddy has something else to tell you."

"Never-na-never-na-never-na-never..." he giggled, bouncing.

"Solin, listen." Kurn said, in a lower tone.

Solin stopped moving and his eyes settled on his father's bent knees.

"Solin, tomorrow — tomorrow you and Mommy are leaving Xianova with Daddy's friends, to a new home."

"Nope."

"Yep. It might be scary at first, but they are going to keep you safe. But Daddy can't come with. Daddy loves you so very much, but there's something I have to do."

"Why, Daddy, WHY?"

"Because I love you, and I love Mommy, and it's the only way to keep you safe."

"No, Daddy! Stay! Stay, Daddy!" Solin punched his father's leg and arm.

Kurn caught his son's fists and held for a moment. He let go, and found Solin watching his face. Tears rolled from Solin's eyes.

"I won't be gone forever, Solin. Daddy will come back to you again someday." Kurn held his breath to stop his own tears, hoping he wasn't lying.

"NO! NevernanevernaNEVER!" Solin screamed, turning to run.

Kurn caught him and pulled him back, hugging him to his chest. Tears burst from his eyes and spilled down his cheeks as his son hugged him back for the first time in his life.

Solin looked up at him quickly, then dropped his eyes. Kurn knew he was about to run.

"Solin, you be a good boy and listen to Mommy, and ONLY to Mommy while I am gone, ok? She loves you and wants to keep you safe. Other people don't understand you like Daddy and Mommy do—"

Solin sucked in his breath and snuffed all the snot he could back into his nose, wiping the rest on his father's bicep. His body was stiff and trembling.

"—And Daddy *will* be back and I'll be *so proud of you* for listening to Mommy and taking care of Mommy. Doing what Mommy says keeps Mommy safe too. You and Mommy keep each other safe. Daddy loves you, and I'm so proud of you, Solin."

Solin's little body stopped trembling and became unnaturally still. He pulled away, staring blankly at the floor. His voice shook. "I didn' like that story, Daddy. It's just a story, right? Just a story."

"It is a terrible story, Solin, but that's how love is sometimes. Remember it. It is a true story."

Solin looked up, his eyes wide. Just for a moment, their eyes locked. Then he ran, shrieking, down the hall.

~3~

From inside the windowless main cabin, Gaspaar heard the recon team greet some of the other men as they approached the camp nestled deep in the Faquir jungle. He hoped they'd been successful. They needed more weapons, and more anti-viral treatment packets for their food. He was excited to hear what they'd found — hopefully not just elk.

He perked up as he heard the door to the supply cabin creak open, and walked over to the front door to unlock it for his men. Then he went back to the map display on the stolen floatscreen he had been looking at earlier. He studied the recent increase in archaeological digs near the southwest arm of the ancient, jungle-devoured Old City. The nearest one was just fifteen miles or so directly to their north, between their camp and the Xianovan dome system.

Working with Coryl had changed the game for them. Before Coryl, they'd been limited to attacking the occasional poorly armed family taking their chances in the jungle to avoid a Blessing. Gaspaar considered it a kindness to put them out of their misery before the nightmare jungle did, but the families rarely had more than a few meager supplies to collect for the trouble. Now, with Coryl's reprogramming help, he and his men were able to take and use restricted weapons from the heavily guarded research teams as well as guard forays from Xianova. In the next few days, he hoped to hit one of the archaeological digs.

Lox opened the door and stepped inside.

Seeing the look on his face, Gaspaar said, "What happened?"

Lox nodded curtly. "Coryl ditched us. We think he helped a target escape."

"What do you mean, 'Coryl ditched us?' Did he head back to Xianova?"

"I don't know, Gaspaar, but he disappeared during the shooting. We searched for like an hour — but he never showed up, and we didn't find his body. We also didn't find where he went. The man is a ghost in the woods. When we staked out the research team, we saw a woman, but we didn't catch her either. We followed her for a while, but she managed to escape. Either she has better survival skills than most, or someone helped her."

"You said you took down the rest of the team — I assume there were guardsmen as well."

"Yes. We got some Teslas, some treatment packets, and plenty of other tech junk that I don't even know what it is. The guys are sorting it out in the storage cabin."

"I know it's getting dark, but we can't afford to have Coryl report back to Xianova on this location. He knows too much. We need to find him and figure out what he's up to. And if necessary, kill him."

"But... Have you seen the man fight? We'll lose people. And if we kill him..."

"We'll just have to use what we have. It's not worth the risk to keep him around if he's a double agent. If he was really with us, he would have kept us in the loop. But if he's with this researcher, maybe she's valuable. Maybe we'll be able to take care of Coryl *and* trade the woman back to our contact in Xianova to get something in return. We'll all go this time. Get everyone, restock, and be ready to head back out in five."

"Some of us just got back; we need—"

"In five."

~4~

Tahni and the giant approached the site where the magnacutter had landed. He crouched down in the vines and overgrowth at the edge of the small clearing; they surveyed the area. The remains of a large fallen tree were visible at the edge of the clearing beyond the magnacutter; a few saplings dotted the clearing, casting shadows in the late afternoon sun. A few thin, broken trunks and a deep skid mark behind the craft indicated an abrupt landing.

She needed to get rid of him. "Hey," she whispered, moving to crouch next to him. "I don't want to risk any more surprises. Could you check the area and make sure we weren't followed? I'll see if anyone's still here, or if the magnacutter is free to be repurposed."

"I'm certain we weren't followed. But I'll check the area anyway. We don't want raiders. Or predators." He backed into the shadows and was soon lost from her sight.

She wasn't sure that was an improvement. Where had he gone, and how long would he be gone?

She swiped up her bio and sent "I'm here — not alone."

Coryl headed away from the woman, doing a cursory job of recon for safety's sake — but he also intended to find out what she was up to. He was sure that she knew the men who had landed here earlier, and that they were still around.

He crept around the clearing and found nothing but a pile of jagmocha scat to indicate the presence of predators or other humans. When he reached the large fallen tree, he edged between the uneven ground and the trunk. After covering himself with a scattering of leaves and debris he'd collected as he walked, he turned on his directional hearing bio-upgrade. With the help of his visor, he could now both see and hear the woman and one of the men talking — from a very safe distance of about 150 feet. They were crouched down next to the magnacutter, but he could see that the man was quite tall and well-built, wearing high-quality jungle attire. These two were Alpha domers.

"He helped you get here—?" the man whispered.

"Yeah, Nyk, but I saw him with the raiders right before that. I don't know what he wants, or why he got me away from them."

Coryl's memory nagged as he listened. He searched his bio's files. *Nyk. Nyk... Ah, that explains it.*

"Well, we don't have much time," Nyk continued. "Should we scrap the plan and try to escape somewhere else?"

"And leave Alaric behind in Xianova? No, there is no chance to turn back on this plan. Xianova — or any other dome — is just as dangerous for Alin as the Faquir."

"Not really — frozen isn't as terrible a death as being killed by raiders, torn limb from limb by a Kong gorilla, dissolved and eaten by a slaughterhound, or..." he shrugged.

"We don't have time for this! We long — LONG — ago decided this was the best option. Too many people are asking pointed questions about Alin now. All it takes is one person to catch me when I swap out an extra sample of Alaric's blood for Alin's — and Alin and I will both be frozen. This *is* the best chance for him to have a life of any kind, especially with Cyril here to help you guys out. While I was doing my trip-planning, I used the drones and satellites to scout for coordinates of places in the Faquir where you guys might be able to set up a secure camp. Here." She tapped her forearm to his to transfer the information, then pulled him in for a quick hug as she peered at the edge of the jungle opposite her, looking almost directly at Coryl's hiding place. "Goodbye. Tell Alin I love him. Now get out of here, before that guy gets back."

He released her. " I know you're right..." He sighed and put his hand through his wavy brown hair. "...But I miss you — and Alaric — already. I just can't believe that God's best plan for our family was to split it in two."

"You know it's not permanent. Someday soon — but after enough time has passed that no one will connect our disap-pearances—"

"Yeah, yeah. I know." He blew out a breath. "Ok." He pulled her back into a crushing hug.

"He's so lucky he has you for a father," she squeezed out against his chest.

"And you for a mother." He kissed her hair, then released her. "We can do this," he said, firmly. "Now what are we going to do about your giant? I can't just leave you here to fend for yourself."

"Don't worry — I'll tell him the magnacutter was deserted, but still functional, and hope he leaves me alone to take it back to Xianova. Maybe he'll come with me, if he's trying to get back there."

They both checked the clearing again. Birds fluttered between branches in the surrounding trees — a good sign.

She continued, "I don't know what I'll tell him about not being able to take it all the way back to the dome, but I'll think of something on the way, maybe a mechanical failure. I'll have to land it in the Old City, or something like that, and blow it up there, somewhere near where the archeologists are taking down some of the unsafe structures, to alleviate suspicion. Then I'll get myself a ride back into Xianova, maybe with one of their transports. That's the best I've come up with. If I get spotted before I get there, or if he's a raider—"

Coryl sighed and swiped his bio, switching off his directional hearing and visor.

There was a very good reason why Xianova didn't trouble itself with Impures who managed to escape the Domes. And a thousand reasons why humanity made its home within the self-contained Dome systems for the last five hundred years.

He *should* leave this woman, and her husband, son, and friend. Right now. Go back to Gaspaar with a really good story and some kind of peace offering — so he could stay alive for his own family's future.

Instead, he got out from under the trunk and sauntered into the clearing. He pretended not to see as Nyk slipped back inside the magnacutter.

~5~

"**K**urn, you don't have to do this. We could all escape together," Noreen pleaded, standing in front of the door of their home.

"You know that I do. The plan requires a heavy distraction, so that guardsmen will be called off of nearby posts, so that you two can be spirited away."

"Who is spiriting us away, again?"

"His name is Joram. He'll find you if you're where you're supposed to be at the right time. He owes me a favor, and he'll get you outside the Dome and deep into the Old City, where you will wait for a man named Coryl to find you. Don't worry — he did it for a living and he is good at finding people. And he will be easy to identify; he's eight feet tall and built like a tank. He promised me he'd get you somewhere in the Faquir where you could start a new life, and to help you get started and learn what you need to know to survive."

"I don't think I can do this! I'm not cut out to be a survivalist. I don't know anything about the jungle! And Solin ignores everything I say. I don't know how I'll keep him safe! He'd be safer being Blessed than staying with me in the Faquir. Maybe we should trust the guidance of the Ministers! Or you just come with us! Don't do this, Kurn. Please."

"You can do this. You're a smart, resourceful woman, and I trust you to take care of our son until I can come back and join you."

"But — there's no guarantee you'll be able to get up there before they find out you have antibodies and assume you're infected. If they find out, you'll be a lab rat, you'll get interrogated — or they'll just kill you outright. And *if* you manage to find Kural among the thousands, and thaw him out, it will take time. How will you keep from being discovered before you can overtake the guards up there? How will you get back without starting a war you can't win? Please, Kurn! Be reasonable! Can't you just evade the guards, and come and join us tomorrow? Your brother is already lost. Don't join him in the stars."

"Don't worry; I have a plan. Yes, it's risky, but I refuse to let my brother rot for 200 years just because he expressed opinions contrary to the Conservator's, and I refuse to let our son suffer the same fate for his condition. I've said goodbye to Solin, and now I'm saying goodbye to you. I can't arouse suspicion today by suddenly *not* being a half hour early to work. Come here."

She came over but did not hug him. She looked at him with a hurt, desperate look in her eyes. All he had time to do was try to make this a proper goodbye. He tilted her face up and kissed her once, gently. He put his arms around her. A tear rolled down his cheek.

Then, he peeled her arms from around his waist, wiped the tear away, and strode out the door as if it were any other day.

~6~

As the giant approached, Tahni made an effort to look like she had just stepped out of the magnacutter. "It's deserted," she said. "I don't suppose you'd let me take it back to Xianova."

"It's not deserted," he replied, hooking his massive thumbs in the straps of his oversized trekpak, and leaning against the scratched-up nose of the magnacutter. "Let's cut to the chase. I know, and have known, about this faked crash-landing since it happened. That's how I knew you were likely headed here before the raiders attacked your team. And I saw you talking to a man I assume is your husband just now."

Tahni glared at him. "I know you were with the raiders; you're one of them."

"That's a bit of a stretch, but yes, I am temporarily cooperating with them, so I can stay alive in the jungle. You may as well tell your husband, son, and friend to come on out here. We have some things to talk about if they are going to survive in the Faquir."

"*IF* I had a family hiding here, why would *you* care about their survival? Wouldn't you just rob us, kill us, and call in your goons to carry off all our supplies? Isn't that how you operate?"

"Don't push it, lady. I saved you from an unmarked constrictor vine and a silverback—"

"Saved yourself. They would have killed you, too."

He stood up, his voice becoming more strained. "If I hadn't been tortured by a deep gut feeling that God was pushing me to help you, I would not be here right now, and you would definitely be dead. You and your husband and friend are Impure by your actions; your son by his defects. You deserve what you get out here, if you choose not to follow the True Path and the guidance of the Conservator."

"And what about you?" Nyk stepped out of the magnacutter to Tahni's dismay. He stepped to her side, and slightly in front of her, pushing her back with his arm. He continued, "Surely you're not claiming to be Pure after participating in the murder of a research party."

"I'm just doing what I can to survive. I had to leave Xianova to protect my family because I asked the wrong question of the wrong person, and it was reported to my superiors. A friend tipped me off that they were coming to Redeem me. I know how to survive out here. I'm endangering my own survival by helping you, yet here I am." He gestured at the surrounding jungle. "I don't think you folks have the same kind of advantages I have. And you brought a kid. Granted, he's a teenager — it must have been nearly impossible, keeping him hidden in Xianova all these years — but based on that information," he made eye contact with her, "I know who you are, Tahni na Keahn-Krienall." He gestured to Nyk, "and Nykoien sur Krienall. By association, and by the cleverness of the fake you just pulled off together, I would guess that your friend's name is...Cyril?"

"What makes you so sure you're right?" Tahni asked, pushing away her husband's protective arm and stepping forward. "There are thousands of people in Xianova." This guy knew way too much. She was glad Cyril and Alin were still relatively safe inside the magnacutter.

"Let's just say that my former line of work involved knowing a lot of things about a lot of people, and I made a few deductions. Your clothes, this magnacutter: you're Alpha dome dwellers. A research trip...." He continued to intently study her face.

She tried to be impassive. "That doesn't make me Tahni or him Nykoien." She shrugged.

He took a step closer, towering over her. "No, but since your groundbreaking work in nanocyte upgrades puts you in a unique position to tamper with genetic samples, and thus conceal your son's disability..."

She held her ground, looking up at an uncomfortable angle. "Why are you so sure he has a disability? If it were that obvious, no genetic sample would save him."

"The only tech guy I know of, in the whole of the Alpha dome, who could pull off a fake explosion that big, then conceal a craft the size of a magnacutter from satellites and drones, *and* completely hack its internal systems to avoid discovery — is Cyril sur Rillion, your lab partner." He paused.

She really couldn't argue with that. Cyril was legendary. She crossed her arms and raised an eyebrow as if she could, though. And glanced at the quickly darkening trees around them.

He backed up to where he could watch them both again. "For this hare-brained plan to pan out at all, you'd need someone with strong survival skills, plenty of experience in the Faquir." He waved his hand toward Nyk. "Conveniently, Tahni was recently divorced from just such a man." He studied Nyk for a reaction.

Nyk didn't break eye contact. "That does sound convenient," he agreed. "But why would he be in cahoots with a woman he'd just divorced?"

"I suspect the divorce was for appearances, part of the elaborate plan to get you and your son out of Xianova without suspicion. Am I wrong?"

"You're in intelligence." Tahni countered, as Nyk and the giant continued their stare-down like a Kong gorilla and a defensive northstar silverback. "A Seraphim."

"Not anymore." He broke eye contact and took another step back, then met Tahni's eyes again.

She frowned. "How can I trust someone who has been kicked out of the Seraphim, the most elite guard in the world — and joined up with raiders, using his knowledge to help them access Teslas so they can plunder more people? That doesn't scream 'trust what he says.'"

He scoffed. "Neither does holding a Minister's position in a genetics lab and tampering with samples for years upon years — or faking a crash to subvert the laws of Xianova, which are guided by the Flawless Word. Yet here we are."

Nyk sighed. He and Tahni shot a questioning glance at each other.

The giant nodded toward the portentous, looming shadow of the Faquir. "We haven't got much time before Gaspaar's men come back. Five hours, maybe. If they catch up, they'll either sell us back to Xianova to be Blessed, or kill us, depending on our perceived value. And yes, they will take all of your supplies, and this magnacutter, which will reveal that your deaths were initially faked, casting plenty of suspicion on all of your family members and friends who remain in Xianova."

Cyril stepped out of the magnacutter, with Alin following, his tall, but thin body shielded behind Cyril's hulk-like body. "Nyk, Tahni. Stop talking. Start moving. Either he's going to stab us in the back or he's not. We won't know until and unless he does. So far, he's been square with us. He said God is telling him to help us. If that's true, then maybe God knows better than we do what we need. His actions to this point, in saving you, Tahni, and his knowledge and intelligence, give us reason to take him with us. And he's right. There's no more time to discuss it."

Alin squatted on the step of the magnacutter, hurled the dagger he'd just finished carving back inside, and grabbed a short nearby fallen branch. His hands visibly trembled as he began shaving the bark with fierce fervor. "I agree," — bark flew in slivers all around him — "with Cyril." He sucked in a breath and sliced a few more times. "This guy may not like me, because I'm different," — more bark fell in a long strand — "but he actually seems pretty honest." Alin glanced up at his parents in turn, his hands briefly pausing. "If he's a Seraphim," he continued slicing another long strand, "then I feel a lot safer than I did about ten minutes ago." *Slice slice slice slice slice...*

Tahni sucked back tears as she watched him carve for a brief moment. She was very glad Alin's whittling was still a strong enough calming activity to keep him from becoming paralyzed with fear, unable to function or speak right now — but as tense as he was, she worried he would cut himself. She stepped closer to the Seraphim operative. "Listen —what's your actual name? Tell us what you need to help us. Later, I want to hear more about how and why you think God told you to help me and my family."

"Name's Coryl. Let's do what you suggested and take the magnacutter back to the Old City, but let's all go together. That'll get us away from here and farther away from Gaspaar, and I'll tell you the rest on the way."

How had he heard that? "Did you somehow tap into my bio?"

He tapped his ear. "Directional hearing upgrade."

She frowned. "Going back to the Old City is like going backwards for us, and it's as dangerous as can be."

"Well, I didn't *ask* you to take me there through Abaddonia," Coryl said, referencing the most feared and deadly part of the Faquir jungle. "But we can go that route if you really want to."

She pursed her lips at him.

He chuckled.

"C'mon," Cyril said. "If we're going to survive out *here*, we can do this. Plus, we need to get you back to Xianova somehow."

Nyk looked at Tahni and curtly nodded his agreement. He swiped his bio and studied it for a minute. "If we can stay just over the tree tops, it will help us avoid detection." He flicked through the images on the screen, studying it intently at times, then flicking away one image for another in frustration. "I don't know how we'll get into the Old City to ditch it without being noticed, but once we do, now that your guards are dead, you'll have to get back to Xianova on your own."

Tahni thought it through. "I'll have to find an archeology crew and lie to them. Tell them I got attacked close to the Old City on my way back."

Coryl nodded. "The Guard will send people to look for your party, and the raiders, but they won't search long nor risk much in the Faquir to find bodies that were likely drug off and devoured." He waved at the magnacutter — the luxury liner of air vehicles — and looked back at Cyril. "Are you sure you can keep *this thing* concealed? And are either of you *that* good a pilot?"

"Pretty sure," Cyril shrugged his own massive shoulders. "I guess you'll have to trust *me* on that one. And Nyk can fly."

Nyk nodded. "Let's get going." He waved everyone toward the door of the magnacutter.

~7~

Kurn met the man as he walked from the residential area, through the main park area, toward the tall, mirror-coated Spires — each designated for a different Ministry's work. The handoff of the experimental vaccine was discreet. A quick stab as he passed in the shift-change crowd. Kurn felt it bubble up under the skin of his upper thigh and kept on walking.

The nausea hit a few steps later, but he kept on. When he got to work, his bio-key was scanned as he approached the door. Instead of opening quickly, the system seemed to be thinking.

I'm screwed if this door can already sense the virus! But — they'll come get me for that, too, I guess. Noreen and Solin will still get out.

He re-submitted his bio-key. This time, the door opened after only a second's hesitation. Kurn let out a controlled breath. Now, to begin a new code set — but *not* for the microscopic nanobots that made up the Dome. Today, he would use his Seraphim credentials to "hack" into the Archangel Gabriel communique system: the system used only by Ministers of Purity to communicate with entire Dome systems at once.

Five minutes later, Kurn's holographic image appeared to everyone in Xianova, hovering above their forearms in place of their bio-implant interfaces. "Friends! Listen! Purity is a sham! The Flawless Word is not Flawless! Friends, *we do not have all of God's Word.* It was pieced together from printed and digital *scraps.* Many, many different translations and interpretations — all slapped together — and called 'Flawless.' How ironic is that, people of Xianova? We have these ideas of what God wants from us, but how do we know they're real?

"One thing I know. We are operating under a *very flawed* system. They don't just give the best stuff to the best stewards; they don't just freeze people with incurable diseases, or criminals, anymore. They give the best stuff to the worst people; they freeze anyone who disagrees with them."

Kurn looked around the room. His coworkers were staring at him in shock. He knew, and they knew, that they might be Redeemed as accomplices if they didn't try to stop him. Any second now...

He added fuel to the fire. "Soon, I'm sure they'll come for me. But before I go, I also want you to know that my supervisor, Dean Jamartin—" he aimed his arm cam at Jamartin's face as it twisted from shock to anger to panic, "is as crooked as they come. If you only knew what he could program a nanobot to do to people he didn't like..." He was interrupted by angry yells and objects flying at him from around the room as his coworkers finally came out of their stupor.

"Stop him!" Jamartin turned and punched the button to call the guardsmen (who were no doubt already on their way, en masse).

Kurn turned his armcam back toward himself and backed slowly toward the door as his coworkers picked up chairs and other furniture as makeshift weapons, and tried to to surround him. "People of Xianova. Don't let your minds be controlled by 'True Path' propaganda! Fight back! Signing off now, so they can Redeem me. If they can catch me." He closed the communique and turned as if to run. Dean Jamartin tackled him as his coworkers closed in.

Kurn fought back...just enough to keep them busy. He needed to be easily accessible, so guardsmen would *not* be sent all over Xianova looking for him.

~8~

Tahni's knuckles were white from her death grip on the armrests of her seat in the magnacutter. She trusted Nyk's piloting skills, but he'd never had to fly like...*this*. She took a deep breath and blew it out, keeping her elbows locked, trying to steady her body (and her stomach) from the constant back-forth-up-down-and-around movement.

Nyk's short beard twitched against his amber skin as he ground his teeth in concentration, zipping sideways and back again between the treetops.

She could do nothing to help him except pray. So she did. Then she turned her seat to face the rear of the compartment.

Cyril's deep umber countenance glimmered with sweat. He slammed his glasses back up his nose with the back of his hand as he worked madly away on his mobile double floatscreen console, probably blinding one satellite after another, feeding them loops of information to conceal their passage. He had one of his huge, muscular legs wedged sideways in the seat to keep himself steady; the see-sawing movement of the magnacutter didn't faze him.

Alin, sitting behind Cyril, was still whittling the stick he'd picked up in the clearing; it was starting to look like a miniature horse. *This was probably not an activity a good mom should allow him to do right now, but...* He braced his thin frame in the seat, brown eyes squinting, long legs crossed around the curved armrest supports. His pile of shavings was spreading around the compartment, but they were going to blow up this vehicle...so the mess didn't matter this time.

She took another mindful breath.

Coryl, from the seat directly behind hers, said, "A little nerve-wracking, isn't it."

She tossed her head over her right shoulder toward Nyk and raised her voice. "Yes, but Nyk's doing a fantastic job."

"Agreed. I'm confident that God will get us through this."

"You keep saying things like that. How are you so sure what God's will is? I'm still wondering — why did you decide to help me?" She turned her seat a few more degrees to face Coryl directly.

"I don't know that I'm ever totally sure of what God's will is. But I have these feelings that just hit me sometimes. So overwhelming that if I try to do something against them, my body is almost paralyzed. Once, I felt like I even heard God's voice, thundering through me. Like a voice I could hear in my thoughts, but that could rip me atom from atom. After that, I just kept digging into the Flawless Word and trying to hear His voice again. To know Him, to know what He wants."

Tahni studied Coryl's face. He appeared to be studying hers, as well, gauging her response. "I don't know that I can tell, either," she said. "But I know what you mean by the feelings. I get them too."

"I got one as we approached your research team earlier. I saw you slip away just as we surrounded your camp, and I knew, very specifically, that I *needed* to follow you, to help you get away."

"I'm glad you did," she said. "I'd be dead if you hadn't. I'd have never seen you coming." She grunted and grabbed the armrest of her seat again as they were violently thrown to one side.

He smiled, righting himself. "Well, I argued with the feeling longer than I should have. I told myself to focus on surviving, so that someday I can reunite with my family with a new identity. But the feeling just got more and more overpowering until I finally just said, 'Ok! Fine!' And went to help you."

Tahni was stunned. A lot of what he said resonated with what was going on in her own life, but unlike her, he hadn't ignored the feelings. She'd been tortured, arguing herself out of the feelings, refusing to be controlled by them. "What about dreams? Do you think He speaks to you in dreams?"

"Well, I read about people in the Flawless Word, and it does make me wonder if God still uses dreams to speak to us. I definitely have a lot of questions, and I want to study the original texts if they can be accessed somewhere. And..." he studied her face again, looking tortured, too.

"And what?" she prompted, leaning back and crossing her leg over her knee, trying to act open and relaxed, instead of riddled with excitement and dread.

"And... I have this weird dream about a girl. Not you, not my wife. I wish I knew what it meant, for sure. I have this completely irrational belief, this rock in the pit of my stomach, that tells me you're connected to it somehow, and that my son's safety — my family's safety — is connected to it. I don't know why." He shrugged, sitting back.

She grinned to cover up the raw emotions forcing their way out through her face. "Yeah, don't worry, you're certifiably weird." She swallowed hard and shifted her rear farther back in her seat, shoving down that same rock in the pit of her own stomach. She wasn't sure what to do now, as they stared at each other in silence; this was more than a coincidence. As a scientist, she often explored her intuitions but hated to feel or look like an illogical person. She couldn't find any helpful logic now, unfortunately. So she changed the subject. "How did you get to be a Seraphim following your feelings and hunches like that?"

"I didn't. I'm normally able to keep my feelings at bay. I like data. I'm dedicated to my cause, and I don't like to take risks — and emotions and intuitions are a risk. But sometimes you can't avoid them. I found that out the hard way when I had my son."

Tahni smiled for real, looking at Alin. "Kids'll do that. For sure. How old is he?"

"Maybe your son's age, or a little older."

Tahni couldn't shake the growing feeling.

He continued, "Having a son definitely changed some things in me. I started to understand how dearly a father protects his son when he loves him. Of course, then I started to really wonder about how God was able to give up his only son to die. I could never do that for someone else. I could sacrifice myself, but not my son."

"Yeah. I feel that. I feel like I'm not good enough for God, because I won't give up my son to be Blessed. I won't follow that law; I just can't sacrifice him. I don't know how Abraham did it."

"Being Blessed isn't really giving him up, is it? Isn't it just selfishness to not let him have a chance at a cure someday, to not trust God with his future?"

"Have you ever known anybody to come back after being Blessed? To me, it's too big of a risk. I lose my son for my lifetime, most likely, and he loses us, and his life on earth, potentially forever, thanks to the Purge."

"Is life, like he is, really a good quality life? In Xianova, if he somehow managed to escape the Blessing, he'd never be considered 'Pure' enough to live in the Alpha dome, even though he's clearly functional in many ways. Your whole family would be affected."

"Is anyone's life without struggle? Why does our particular brand of struggles make us better than him? Why would God ask me to give him up, just because he has a disability?"

Coryl turned and studied Alin for a few seconds.

Her boy, almost a man now, stopped whittling and looked back at him, meeting his eyes only briefly. "I *can* hear you, you know. I'm not deaf. You talk about me like I don't exist or understand, but I do. I understand better than most what it means to *not* be considered 'Pure enough,' but I don't care. I like who I am, even though I struggle with a lot of things. And I love being with my family and living my life. Do you ever wonder why we are expected to strive to be so Pure?"

"Yes. I do," Coryl answered him. He turned back to Tahni. "You both make good points. And I've thought about some of this, just not from your specific angle. It's kind of why I had to leave Xianova. I know that God loved us before we were born and that we didn't have to do anything to get that love — just like my son didn't have to do anything to earn my love. I wouldn't want my son to care so much about being 'perfect' that he couldn't care about anything else. Just to do his best. So that's what I'm trying to do for God. My best."

"I've—" she stopped. She barely knew this guy. But she was overcome with the need to *tell him*. She hadn't even mentioned this to Nyk yet. Not really.

"What?"

"I've...also had a weird dream. About a — girl. Several times, each time slightly different, like a different angle on her, but the same situation. It's very vivid."

He sat forward, almost involuntarily, as the magnacutter came to an almost complete stop, then started again. "Tell me about it." He continued to grip his armrests unnecessarily firmly. His body was tensed like a leopard above an antelope.

Cyril's tapping and swiping on both his bio and the floatscreens gained speed and ferocity. So did Alin's knife.

She still couldn't help it. Bracing herself between her armrests again, she continued. "She's young, only in her teens. Getting Redeemed as she leaves the same school my sons go to."

"Describe her," he ordered.

Her stomach flipped. She could barely get the words out. "Muscular. Tall. And her hair — auburn, almost *red*."

He sat back, pulling on his beard and thinking for a moment. His face was still flushed with excitement, though. Meeting Tahni's gaze directly again, he said, "In *my* dream, I don't see her hair or how tall she is. I only see her face, which is pale, very fair skin. But her eyes are—"

"Green!" Tahni shouted. The magnacutter suddenly jarred upwards, over the treetops, and stopped. Cyril looked up, briefly, and Alin stared at her.

"DON'T DO THAT!" Nyk shuddered and took a breath. "You made me think I was going to hit something!"

"Sorry," Tahni said. "I'm sorry. But we may have been seeing the same woman—"

"Tell me about it later!" he said, resuming his course downward, back into the treetops.

She looked back at Coryl.

"Yes, green eyes in my dream, too."

"What happens in *your* dream?"

"Not much. She looks at me. She looks at me, like she's pleading with me, or asking me questions I don't want to answer. And I know that she holds the future of my family in her hands. There's some kind of barrier between us; she can't seem to understand what I'm saying."

"In mine, the guardsmen take her in front of her peers, at my sons' school — which is weird — a girl with reddish hair, green eyes, and fair skin in the Alpha dome? How did she get to be my sons' age without getting sent down some levels, or even Redeemed? And I know she can resist. She has what looks like a jagmocha with her. For real, in the Alpha dome — a jagmocha."

He put a hand up to pause her. "There *is* actually a jagmocha being raised and trained in the Alpha dome right now."

She sat back, shivering even though she was physically sweating. "People look scared of them, as you might expect. But she goes to her knees and submits. And I feel this sense of dread, like if they take her, something very terrible will happen to *literally everyone in Xianova*. There is this sense of *importance* around her. Maybe she's symbolic. I don't know how to describe it, but in my dream, I just *know* she's the key to something big. "

"The key to saving Xianova from something terrible."

"Yes."

"I don't see any of that in my dream, but I do have a sense of *vital* importance about her. And dread. The feeling I had — that you are connected to this dream. I guess if we're having the same one, you *are* connected."

"Can't really deny that now, can I." She laughed. Emotions seemed to be bubbling out of her now. Tears welled up. Her body felt like it was molten. She was both terrified and excited that there was something *to* her dream for real.

"I think it's more than *just* a connection. But assuming we're dreaming about the same woman, and these feelings are from God, what do we do about it?"

Tahni uncrossed her legs and stretched, trying to ease her tension. "I have absolutely no idea. What would *you* propose we do about it? What do you think it means?"

The magnacutter zipped into the canopy and the windows went dark. Nyk slowed down but kept moving. Branches squealed along the side of the magnacutter and broke off as he swerved through them.

He sat back and stared out the window. "I don't know. I've never tried to interpret a dream. Most of my life, that all seemed like ancient hocus-pocus to me. But I don't believe in coincidences anymore, so I think we are together for a reason, that this is a message. I guess we should pray for wisdom and see what happens."

"Yeah, I mean... You said there *was* a jagmocha. What if...?"

"Maybe when you get back, you watch for this girl, and if somehow you find her, you could pass whatever you find out to me through your husband. I have no idea how you two plan to communicate in the future, but I assume you've got a plan. For my part, I guess I'm working with you guys to help you survive now, too."

Tahni got shivers up her spine. "Ok then."

"I'm super happy you two dreamers have connected on this deep level," Nyk said over the sounds of more branches breaking as he angled up toward the treetops again. "But when we get there, we're going to need a plan. Perhaps you guys could dream up one of those?"

"Actually," Coryl looked embarrassed, "I need your help with something when we get there."

"How can we help *you*?" Nyk asked. "Didn't you say our plan was hare-brained, and that we wouldn't survive on our own?"

"Well, to be honest, you've already saved me once by taking me with you. But I was already planning to keep going north, leaving the rest of the recon team to head back south to camp with the stuff we took. Gaspaar wants to raid some sites in the Old City, so I was conveniently going on a quote-unquote 'hunting and recon' trip to 'scout the area.' That plan was shot to hell when I helped Tahni escape...but either way I need to be in the Old City by tonight."

"Why?" Nyk glanced back at him for a nanosecond.

"The friend that helped me get out of Xianova wanted something in return; he made me promise to find his wife and son, who would be delivered to a certain location in the Old City on this date, and to stay with them and protect them until they could fend for themselves or until I could find another way for them to escape."

"So what do you want from us?" Cyril asked. "You want us to take care of them?"

"Right now, I could just use some help in getting away from Gaspaar's crew, finding them, and getting them out of the Old City. They may be dead already; the Old City is not a safe place, as I'm sure you are keenly aware." He shrugged and looked out the windows again. "We can go from there with the plans."

Nyk sighed. Without looking back, he punched the air with a thumbs-up, then went back to frowning at the digitized overlay of the treetops as he attempted to stay on course.

"I hope we can find that poor little boy before he gets eaten," Cyril said.

"Me too," Coryl said.

"You might wanna give me those coordinates, then," Cyril pointed out. "I'll send the new course to Nyk."

"Why isn't your friend coming to join his family?" Tahni asked, as Coryl swiped his bio and tapped forearms with Cyril.

"He's getting himself Redeemed today as a distraction."

~9~

M *ommy is distracted. Mommy doesn't know what to do. I*
don't know where we are. Why are we here? Daddy said
we leave Xianova today with Daddy's friends. But Daddy's friend
left us here in this dark place all alone.

Mommy doesn't know what to do. She is crying. She is mad.

"Daddy will be back soon, Mommy."

"No, Solin, Daddy will not be back soon. No one comes back
from the stars."

"Daddy said sometimes they do."

"Daddy — wanted to make us feel better. But Daddy knows no
one ever comes back."

"Why, Mommy? Why? Daddy said he was coming back. Daddy
doesn't lie. Daddy told me to listen to you, and do what you say,
and protect you, and he'd come back soon. Daddy doesn't lie."

"You don't have to protect Mommy, Solin. Mommy needs to
protect you. Let's talk about this later. Mommy needs to figure out

how to keep us both safe. It's not very safe here, but we're waiting for Daddy's friend Coryl to come and get us, and he'll protect us. Come here, and I'll hold you."

"No NO NO! NO NO NO! No holding!" Solin ran to the other side of the dark, cave-like ancient room. Moonlight squeezed through a small, broken-open hole there. Outside this cave, it mostly looked like dark, dirty, tangled jungle mess.

I hope he comes soon. I hope he comes soon. It's scary and dark here. Why did Daddy leave? So scary. Animal eyes? Solin inched closer, hoping the thing couldn't see him. He could smell something. Something very bad.

Icky gross stinky dead animal there. It is looking at me. Staring. Why? Why is the icky gross thing staring at me like that? It's dead. Right? Not moving. Maybe not dead. Going back by Mommy.

"Good boy, Solin. Come back to Mommy. It's scary here, but Mommy's working on a plan to keep us safe."

"Stinky stinky stinky stinky dead dead dead," he whispered, shaking.

"What?"

"Over there."

"Oh. It's dead, Solin. Yes. And very stinky."

"What if it's not."

"Dead?"

"What if it's not dead."

"It's dead, Solin, honey. We only have to worry if what killed it comes back for it — but I don't think it will. It's been there a long time, and nothing's bothered it. That's probably a good sign."

"He better come soon."

"He will."

"Is Daddy going to be dead dead dead like the animal?"

"Oh, Solin. Not like that."

"*WHAT WILL WE DO WITHOUT DADDY?!*" Solin
screamed and kept screaming. The whole world seemed darker,
totally black. He could hardly see Mommy at all. Only the stars,
laughing at him, keeping Daddy forever.

"I don't know! Hush, Solin, I don't know! That's why Mommy
is crying and mad. He left us alone. But Mommy will figure it out!
I will figure it out! I promise. But you have to be quiet here. Hush
now. We'll be ok."

All he could see was the dead thing's eyes, staring at him from
every direction now. And suddenly, the dead thing's eyes turned
into Daddy's eyes. Staring at him from the dark, from the sky,
from everywhere. He gagged and choked. A few seconds later, he
repeated, still very loudly, "All alone. No Daddy. No! Daddy said
he's coming back. He's coming back, right, Mommy?"

"Solin, honey, take a breath, try to be quiet and just be here with
Mommy, ok? Let's look for the big man who is coming to protect
us. His name is Coryl. Let's look for Coryl now."

"He's coming soon, Mommy."

"Ok, Solin. Ok."

~10~

It had taken Coryl three days to find Kurn's wife — much too long. Part of that was because she was not where she was supposed to be. She had chased the little boy hysterically through that portion of the Old City — between and over piles of dirt, scrub, and tangled cement rubble and steel the size of small mountains; through sunken, half-excavated, or overgrown rooms; into small, buried, cave-like buildings; through a grassy field or two...and into a completely different area of the Old City, losing her own way in the process. With angels protecting them, apparently, because they'd managed to avoid being killed by constrictor vines or roving predators. If Gaspaar guessed where they'd gone or carried out his plan to raid in the area, and hadn't picked up their trail by now, he'd for sure heard the boy screaming several different times. They'd be lucky if the people at the dig sites hadn't heard him and sent guards to investigate.

Coryl had no idea how he was going to keep this boy and his mother safe in the Faquir, where the wrong noise at the wrong time would get you killed and eaten before you could stop screaming.

First, though, they had to figure out how to get Tahni back to the Dome without ruining her alibi. *Yeah, should have done that first!* But they didn't have time.

Nyk had the boy, Solin, on his shoulders, which kept him quieter and entertained for the moment. Alin was visibly, and sometimes audibly, frustrated and angry with the boy, and Coryl couldn't really blame him; Solin was endangering them all with his noises.

Coryl looked at his bio, which had far more capability than the average Xianovan's. He turned and signaled a course correction in the direction of the nearest active dig site. The boy's mother, Noreen, and Tahni were right behind him as he started working his way through a narrow gap between walls of fallen debris in the jungle-overgrown ruins.

Single file, they squeezed through the gap. On the other side, there was a small open meadow, with four-foot-tall grass and weeds blowing in the breeze. Anything could be in there.

He scanned the field for a full minute, and then the edge of the Faquir jungle next to it. Something was wrong. A flash of metal in the sun. "Get down!"

Tahni and Noreen flung themselves down, but Nyk and Solin made it through the gap a second too late. A Tesla blast zinged by Solin's left leg, and he screamed from the searing pain. Nyk swept the boy from his shoulders and dropped to the ground, covering

Solin's mouth. Cyril and Alin stayed in the gap, crouching low to blend with the shadows.

"They found us," Coryl whispered to Nyk. "Ideas? We can't get back through there fast enough to avoid being killed. If we head into the field, they'll see the grass moving. If we stay here..."

"Gotta be the field. We need to split up, flank them, maybe."

"Go that way with Tahni." Coryl pointed north and motioned for Noreen to follow him, with Solin.

"Wait!" Cyril called, softly. "Better plan." He was rifling through his oversized trekpak. A second later, he pulled out a tank drone.

"Are you kidding me?" Coryl said. "When did you have access or clearance for a *tank drone?*"

"It's one that I may, or may not have, reassembled from parts I have collected over the years."

"Does it work?"

"Does — it — work?!" Cyril peered over the top of his wire-rimmed glasses.

"Long shot at best," Gaspaar's voice boomed over their whispers, as he stood up in the grass not ten feet from where they were. "Cobbled-together tank drone? That thing could just as easily blow us all up as do what you want it to do. Stand up. Put your hands up, all of you."

"Hellll no!" Cyril said. "This baby is *upgraded*. She can take the eyelashes off a fly, or take out this whole field if your men don't get smart and show themselves."

A few of Gaspaar's men started to stand up. He waved them back down. He pointed his charged Tesla at Cyril. "Not before I shoot you." The Tesla's soft whine seemed to be the only sound in the world for a few seconds. The roar of a distant cat — leopard, probably — broke the silence.

Nyk stood up, splitting the distance between the two men, and raised a hand to each of them. "No one needs to die. Maybe we can work together."

"Work with you...to do *what*? You have women and children here. They're a liability. I'm not a babysitter. Neither are my men."

"I can cook, in exchange for protection for my son and I," Noreen said.

"And Alin there has learned to hunt and track, and has a knack for it," Nyk said, indicating his son, who stood behind Cyril.

"Or I just kill you and that woman and these kids, and then sell Researcher Girl, Tank Drone Guy, and Coryl to my contact in Xianova — for enough supplies to last us for months. Problem solved."

Coryl growled, "I *guarantee* that you'd be better off killing me than selling me back to Xianova—"

Noreen interrupted, "Look, why wouldn't you want to keep 'Tank Drone Guy' alive? Imagine what he could do with some scavenged tech from Xianova. And if you had, say, a mobile tent-dome, we'd all be safe from both predators in the jungle and satellites above."

"That only saves Tank Drone Guy."

Pointing to Tahni, Noreen continued, "You want us all. Tahni here, like me, cares about her family's safety in the Faquir. She's a vital supply chain link, but only if you take her family with you. I can cook, like with real game and wild herbs, because my husband brought them back from his excursions. But I also have helpful contacts in Xianova, among the guardsmen, if you take my son and I."

Coryl looked at Noreen and raised an eyebrow.

Gaspaar shook his head. "You all talk a good game. But Coryl already ditched us once to run off with you folks. Trust and loyalty are what counts."

Coryl threw up his hand. "Gaspaar, if I was going back to Xianova, I could have done it months ago. She's right. We're all more valuable to you alive."

Nyk added, "Tahni has already proven her worth as a link to Xianova. She made a farce of a research trip to find us, so she could give us drone-scouted information about safer locations to start out in the Faquir. Which we could share with you."

Noreen indicated the jungle. "You might not need to do what you do, at least not quite so often — if you had a viable mobile tent-dome and a better supply chain of information and supplies from Xianova."

"I heard your kid screaming from literally a mile away. There's no way I'm risking death because he can't keep his mouth shut. Who's in charge of that?"

As if on cue, Solin began shrieking. Noreen clamped a hand over his mouth. "He's a handful, but he's extremely smart. He'll learn. Yes, stuff is going to happen with him that might put some of us in danger — but I'm not asking *you* to die for him if it comes to that. We can more than pull our weight in the meantime."

"Make up your minds," Cyril said. "Is this going to be a standoff? Or are we working together? I'm good either way." He rubbed his thumb over the small remote he was holding, and the tank drone closed the fifteen or twenty feet between Cyril and Gaspaar in less than a second.

Gaspaar's men slowly stood up behind him. Lox put his hands up and chucked his Tesla toward Nyk. "I prefer having a tank drone on *my* side." A few of the other men threw their Teslas toward Nyk and Coryl as well.

Gaspaar dropped his gun. "Pointing a tank drone at them may change their minds *for now*. I'll go along with it — and you all — *for now*. But you better keep an eye on that kid. He makes a peep, I'll shoot him myself."

Cyril backed the tank drone off a few feet.

Noreen nodded, but when Gaspaar picked up his gun again and turned away from her, she glared daggers at him.

"You'll probably want these back now," Nyk said, tossing the Teslas back to the men who had thrown them.

Gaspaar assumed control as if he had never lost it. "Coryl, get Research Girl over to the dig site so she can hitch a ride. Since guardsmen will likely be swarming the area tomorrow, by morning we need to be miles away. That means traveling the Faquir at night. Hope you're all up for that." He waved to his men, and they quickly disappeared again, heading for the jungle, barely ruffling the grass.

"Bye Mom," Alin said. "I wish you were coming with us."

Tahni hugged him, and Nyk threw his arms around both of them. "I love you, Alin," Tahni said. "So very much. Maybe someday soon we can all be together again. But I think with Coryl's help, I can at least find a way to see you in the jungle sometimes. Love you too, dear. I'm really going to miss you both." Nyk kissed her, and as she pulled away from them, tears started down her cheeks. She quickly wiped them away and looked at Coryl.

Nyk looked at Coryl too. "Make sure she gets there."

"I will, don't worry. You'll both see her again. Keep an eye on Noreen and Solin for me, and don't turn your back on Gaspaar or any of his men. Not one of them is likely to honor their pact for long."

"I gathered that," Nyk said. "But at least we got this far, today. Survival is one day at a time...and so is trust."

"I'll catch up to you tomorrow." He waved Tahni along. "Let's go — the faster we get there, the faster I get back to them."

~11~

Twilight was just starting to shimmer through the transparent-but-deadly nanite web that protected Xianova as Tahni opened the door to her house and walked in. She was so happy to be home. And safe.

And so unhappy.

"Mom!" Alaric called, relief visible on the face that was nearly identical to the one she'd just said goodbye to the night before. He hugged her tightly and then released her. "How was your *trip*?"

"Pretty scary...some raiders hit the research party as we were headed back into Xianova, but I managed to make it back to a dig site in the Old City and they helped me get home."

He looked worried, but she'd trained him to be discreet when discussing the plan. She nodded silently, and a tear escaped. He hugged her again. "They're safe, for now," she whispered in his ear. "More help than they counted on, but it might not all be helpful. We can only pray and hope until the next time I can get out there.

Dad and Alin send their love." She stepped back again and changed her tone. "Enough about that; I'm alive and I'm back safe, and that's good enough for now. How was school?"

"Well, pretty normal," he said, stepping into the open kitchen area behind them. "There was one thing that happened today, though, that I'm sure you'll hear about."

"Did you get into trouble?" She frowned at him.

"Dinner's on me tonight," he said, and handed her a food cube from the dispenser in the kitchen with a glass of water.

"Whoa, you went all out," she said, popping it in her mouth and chewing the lasagna-flavored, noodle-textured mass as it expanded with the water she drank. She swallowed. "Now. Seriously. I'm not going to get any back notifications—"

"No, Mom! It wasn't me. This girl, some people were picking on her out on the green before school, calling her ugly. She literally kicked their butts. The whole group. She had *skills*, Mom. Like she must have been training for years already, or something."

"Fighting is not the best way to solve a problem," Tahni answered, taking a drink. She gazed out the window at her roses, her thoughts crowding in. A second later, it clicked. "Wait, who did you say got in trouble?"

"I don't know her name," he said, chewing, "but I know she got sent down for Spiritual Blessings because of it. She maybe could have *not* kicked their butts, but I bet they won't be calling anyone else ugly for a while. Definitely not *her*," he chuckled. "I was kinda rooting for her when I heard it. I didn't tell anybody that, though."

"Why were they calling her ugly?" She sat down in her favorite chair and sipped her water.

"Somebody was saying she's all washed out like a vampire, because her skin's so light, and green eyes are a sign of impurity. Somebody else said she was too tall for a girl; maybe she's a boy in disguise." He gulped down the end of his water and burped.

She gave him a disapproving look.

He smiled. "Then she said something like—" he affected a 'tough girl' voice and posture — "'I may be too tall, and not pretty, but you're welcome to come get a closer look so you can be sure I'm a girl — and then I'll take you to the ground in thirty seconds or less.' And they said, 'Prove it!' so she did. And she told them to be sure to pass on to their parents that it was, indeed, a girl that beat them up." He took her cup from her and brought both of their cups to the kitchen sink.

Tahni had goosebumps. "What color was her hair?"

"Why does that matter? I have no idea. I didn't actually see it happen. People were just talking about it. That was the most interesting thing that's happened at school in years. Plus, I thought it was funny."

Funny, indeed.

For More Adventures in the World of Xianova...

Read *The Frozen!*

ABOUT THE AUTHOR

Jen Porter is an award-winning educator and author who promotes faith and interdependence. Jen and her husband Jim live in Cedar Rapids, Iowa — with family, fish, jealous and paranoid rescue dogs, plenty of 'Dad' jokes, and never enough *Star Trek*.

GET THIS EBOOK
...and other sci-fi and fantasy books and stories
FREE!

Grab a free monthly subscription to *The Blessed Bulletin* here:

JEN PORTER